YOGI BEAR™

HOME SWEET JELLYSTONE

STORY ADAPTED BY DANDI MACKALL & SCOTT AWLEY
COVER ILLUSTRATION BY GITA LLOYD
PENCILS BY IWAO TAKAMOTO
INTERIOR ILLUSTRATIONS BY DARRYL GOUDREAU

Yogi Bear and Boo Boo watched as a car chugged through the gate at Jellystone National Park. "It's a messenger from the telegraph office, Boob!" said Yogi. "It might be for me!"

"Who'd send you a telegram, Yogi?" asked Boo Boo.

"How would I know till I opened it, Boo Boo?"

"Right over here, Boy!" Yogi called.

But the messenger whizzed past Yogi in a cloud of dust. "Get lost, ya dusty old bear!" cried the messenger.

Yogi brushed off the dust. "A little dusty perhaps, but not old!"

Inside the park office, Ranger Smith opened his telegram. "This is one telegram Yogi didn't read first!"

"I hope it isn't bad news, Chief," said his assistant.

"Listen to this!" And the Ranger read aloud: *"Chief Ranger Smith, you are heir to your late Uncle Charlie's fortune. Provision states you must live in his mansion to qualify."*

"Do you know what that means?" said the Ranger.
"No more babbling brooks! No more finding lost kids or putting
out forest fires! And above all, NO MORE YOGI BEAR!"

"You called, Sir?" Yogi asked through the cabin window.

"Yes, Yogi," answered the Ranger. "I'd like you to read this
telegram."

"See, Boob?" Yogi said proudly. "Mr. Ranger can't make a
move without me."

Yogi read the telegram in disbelief. "But Mr. Ranger! It means you're leaving the park!"

"I m leaving you, Yogi. You've caused me nothing but trouble and made my life miserable! You are a bad bear!"

"Since we're leveling, Sir, we bears were here first and got along better without you Rangers!" exclaimed Yogi.

"Well! I'm glad to know how you feel about me, Yogi. Good riddance! If I never see another bear, it'll be too soon!"

Yogi and Boo Boo watched the Ranger drive away.
"I'm going to miss Mr. Ranger, Yogi," said Boo Boo.
"Me too, Little Buddy — like ya miss a toothache!
Hee-yuh-hay! Come on — let's raid those pic-a-nic tables!"

Mr. Ranger sat alone in his mansion. "Ahh, this is the life! No worries. Not like that windy Jellystone Park! Still...two weeks without a single letter. Well, if they don't miss me, I won't miss them!"

Back at Jellystone Park, nothing seemed the same for Yogi and Boo Boo. "Ranger's been gone a month, two days, and six hours, Boo Boo," said Yogi.

"Maybe a picnic basket would cheer you up, Yogi," suggested Boo Boo.

"Ee-e-ech!" Yogi pointed to a pile of picnic baskets. "It's too easy since Mr. Ranger left, Boob. I miss the battle of wits. The Ranger was a worthy adversary!"

"But Yogi, you haven't eaten for days! You might get sick!"

"Don't worry, Boob! It's all part of my scheme to get Mr. Ranger back!"

Boo Boo and Yogi eavesdropped outside the Ranger's cabin.
"He's talking to Mr. Ranger, Boo Boo," whispered Yogi.

"Boo Boo's fine," the Ranger's assistant was saying. "But
it's sad about Yogi. He hasn't eaten for weeks!"

"That ought to do it, Boo Boo!" Yogi said. "Hey, hey, hey!
Let's be on our way!"

"Where to, Yogi?" Boo Boo asked.

"To meet Mr. Ranger, of course!"

The worried Ranger raced out of his mansion and headed straight for Jellystone National Park. All the way he muttered to himself, "Poor Yogi, dragging himself around the forest! Of course, I'd come to the rescue of any dumb animal."

"How do you know Mr. Ranger will come, Yogi?" Boo Boo asked.

"Because Mr. Ranger is one of the good guys, Boob. And here he is now!"

As the Ranger drove through Jellystone gate, Yogi threw himself in the road and moaned. "I know that voice from somewhere," Yogi said weakly. "It's that nice Mr. Ranger! How are you, Sir?"

Mr. Ranger rushed to Yogi's side. "Oh, you poor bear!" the Ranger cried. "I should never have left you, Yogi, but I'm back! I'll have you up and around in no time! Lots of rest and good food will do it!"

The Ranger heaved Yogi over his shoulder.
"How about pic-a-nic baskets, Sir?" Yogi asked.
"Sure, Yogi," said Ranger. "Until you get your strength back."
"Hey, hey, hey!" muttered Yogi Bear. "This could be the longest convalescence of all time!"

"There's one thing you gotta admit about Yogi," said Boo Boo. "For a dumb animal, he's smarter than the average Ranger!"